The Everys

The Everys

Cody Lee

Long Day Press

Chicago

Published by Long Day Press
Chicago, Il 60647
LongDayPress.com
@LongDayPress

ISBN: 978-1-950987-15-3

Library of Congress Control Number: 2021934941

Edited by Joseph Demes
Designed by Joshua Bohnsack

Cover Image: Figures
by Auguste Rodin

Printed in the United States of America
First Edition

Contents

<u>COLD OPEN</u>

FADE IN:

INT. STARBUCKS - DAY

BAILEY, 25, dressed business casual, stands in line at Starbucks. Instead of a "normal" head, Bailey has a head made of gray clay. It is circular and has stripes of color tucked into its creases. Bailey's skin is gray too. They have no distinct race or gender.

Bailey is the only one in Starbucks that looks like this. No one seems to notice any difference.

While Bailey waits, the **BARISTA**, early 30s, yells names like *Chuck*, *Bella*, and *Chris*. One by one, Chuck, Bella, and Chris go up to the bar and grab their drinks.

When Bailey makes it to the front of the line, the **CASHIER**, late teens, is smiling.

CASHIER

Hello.

BAILEY

Hey, how are ya'? I'll just do a tall cappuccino.

CASHIER
No problem! It'll be three seventy-two.

Bailey hands the cashier four dollars, puts the change in the tip jar, then waits again. More names like *Dustin*, *Chelsea*, and *Kayla* are called. Then...

BARISTA
Cappuccino!

Bailey approaches the bar.

BAILEY
For me?

BARISTA
I don't know. There's no name on it.

After a pause, Bailey takes the cup.

BARISTA
Jeanine! Jeanine Humphries, your
coffee's at the bar!

Bailey thinks about saying something, doesn't. As they're leaving, **JEANINE**, early 40s, blonde, runs up to Bailey.

JEANINE
Hey, I think you took my cappuccino by
accident.

BAILEY
Oh, are you sure?

JEANINE
I think I'd know my own cappuccino.
Here, this one's yours.

Jeanine hands Bailey a cup with red lipstick all over the mouth hole.

BAILEY
Uh... Okay.

Bailey and Jeanine switch cups and start to leave. Jeanine exits first. The door swings back, spilling a little coffee on Bailey's shirt.

FADE OUT.

<u>END OF COLD OPEN</u>

<u>ACT ONE</u>

FADE IN:

INT. SIMPLE CORP. - DAY

Bailey enters the Simple Corp. building. The lobby is clean and spacious. Everyone is dressed business casual. Bailey waves to the man at the front desk, who doesn't wave back.

They squeeze into a full elevator. Everyone besides Bailey is wearing a name tag. One person is listening to Black Flag too loud on their headphones. Another person is eating olives straight from the jar.

Bailey gets off on the 16th floor, a large space with a hundred cubicles. The lights are painfully fluorescent.

Bailey walks past the cubicles, all the way to the back. There's a hook where they hang their jacket. Above the hook, a gold nameplate reads: *Ass Kisser*.

There's a water fountain by the hook, too, and a large window overlooking Navy Pier.

Bailey checks their watch, 8:59. They lift a long feather

from inside their shirt pocket, inspect it, then put it back in. They pull a stick of lip balm out of the same pocket and apply a little too much. They pucker their lips ten times. Touch their toes. Crack their knuckles. Stretch their face.

They walk over to the first cubicle, labeled: *P. Stetson*. Bailey knocks on the styrofoam paneling. Once, twice, three times. **PHILIP STETSON**, 40s, Black, is inside misting a small plant. When he notices Bailey, he waves them in.

Philip stands up. Bailey nods to him, he nods back. [Beat] Philip turns around, unbuckles his pants, and drops them to the floor, underwear included. His butt cheeks are hairless.

Philip points to the left one. Bailey approaches, drops to both knees. They breathe, pucker up, then plant one gentle, suspenseful kiss on Philip's butt cheek.

As Bailey pulls away slowly, their lips stick to Philip's skin, leaving an imprint from all of the balm.

Bailey stands and Philip pulls his pants back up. Bailey leaves without either of them saying anything.

Bailey knocks three times on the cubicle next door, labeled: *F. Vogt*. **FRANCESCA VOGT**, 30s, white, with a half-shaved head and a deep voice, is teary-eyed and slouching in her chair. She is holding a framed photo of her and another woman. When Francesca notices Bailey, she wipes her face.

FRANCESCA
Sorry. Uh. My wife died last night.
Aneurysm. But the rent's not gonna
pay itself now will it? Ha! You know,
I think I'll uh... I think I'll switch it up
today. Let's go right cheek. Yeah, feelin'
spontaneous.

Francesca stands, turns around, and pulls her pants
down. Bailey gets on both knees and kisses her right
butt cheek. They can feel her crying, so they rest their
head against her lower back and hold her.

While Bailey is holding her, Francesca farts. Bailey
stands, leaves without saying anything.

They knock on the next cubicle, labeled: *M.
Fleischmann*. Inside, **MICHAEL FLEISCHMANN**, 50s,
white, with a toupee and a squeaky voice, is man-
spreading without any pants on. His long shirt covers
his groin.

MICHAEL
Where is it? Hm? I'm telling you right
now, Ass Fuck, you better not take
another step if you forgot the goddamn
feather again! I am not in the mood!

Bailey pulls the feather out of their pocket. Michael
stands, turns around, and spreads his cheeks.

MICHAEL
I don't have all day!

Reluctantly, Bailey walks up behind Michael and starts tickling his asshole with the feather.

INT. MR. DUMONT'S CLASSROOM - DAY

NICKY, 14, clay head in the shape of a star, sits at their desk, which is situated in the middle of twenty-five other desks (arranged five by five). Nicky's youth is made apparent by their soft, innocent eyes and the lack of wrinkles in their gray face.

Nicky is dressed in a flannel and black jeans, with chipped red nail polish. Everyone around them is dressed equally as casual.

The classroom walls are decorated with posters of Henry David Thoreau, James Baldwin, and Emily Dickinson.

MR. DUMONT, early 30s, a beautiful white man, stands in front of the class. He presses play on the SMART Board, playing "Claymation" by Mac Miller.

Once the chorus is finished, he stops the song.

>   **MR. DUMONT**
> Okay, class. What was Mr. Miller talking about?

The entire class stares at Nicky.

>   **MR. DUMONT (CONT'D)**
> Anyone?

Nicky sinks into their seat.

MR. DUMONT (CONT'D)
Nicky? Anything to contribute? Notice any specific... motifs?

Silence.

MR. DUMONT (CONT'D)
Okay, I'll pose another question. Rap. Poetry. What's the difference? [Beat] I'll tell you what the difference is. Bullshit. You know what I'm talking about, right LaQuan?

LAQUAN, 14, Black, stares blankly. The bell rings and everyone starts to leave.

MR. DUMONT
Remember the homework! There is none! Ha ha. Just make sure you all go to the basketball game. Support your school and your classmates. Good luck out there, Nicky. We'll be watching! LaQuan, make sure you pass the ball this time.

LAQUAN
I'm not on the team!

INT. LOCKER ROOM - DAY

Nicky is in a unisex locker room with the rest of the basketball team. They're wearing a white, long-sleeved compression shirt and red and blue basketball shorts. Nicky's legs are gray.

They reach into their locker and grab their jersey, put it on. The back of it says: NICKY. None of the other players have names on their jerseys.

COACH NASSO, mid 30s, an athletic Middle Eastern woman, enters the locker room.

      COACH NASSO
  Alright team, gather 'round!

The team huddles in front of the coach.

     COACH NASSO (CONT'D)
  I've said everything I could say, done
  everything I could do. If there's not a
  fire burning in your heart right now, I
  don't want you to step foot onto that
  court. The whole school's out there:
  dweebs, cool kids, even some of the
  teachers. We all know who they came
  to see. Give 'em a show. You got that?
  Give 'em a show. Nicky, get us goin'.

Nicky starts humming. The other players follow suit. Some caw. Others howl. Before long, they're all screaming.

Nicky leads the team through a fog machine and onto

the court. The stadium is packed and the school's band is playing. Nicky does a cartwheel. The fans cheer. Some hold signs that say: I LOVE YOU NICKY! Others wear gray, star-shaped masks.

The players grab basketballs and practice layups while Nicky runs around the court, hyping up the crowd.

INT. BOOKSTORE - DAY

REESE, 60, clay head in the shape of a triangle, sits in a comfortable chair in a bookstore, reading a detective novel. There are wrinkles in their face. Reese has a large masculine build, but the voice of a woman. They are dressed in a crewneck sweater and blue jeans.

Customers of all ages and ethnicities browse the store.

Reese makes eye contact with the **OWNER**, early 60s, a delicate white woman. She nods almost imperceptibly.

EXT. BOOKSTORE - CONTINUOUS

Reese follows the woman outside, into an alley. The woman hands them a hundred dollar bill.

> **REESE**
> Thanks.

> **OWNER**
> No, thank *you*! Seriously. Great job today.

Reese smiles, then starts to walk away. The owner grabs them by the arm.

> **OWNER**
> You have no idea the impact you've made.

> **REESE**
> Just doin' my job.

> **OWNER**
> Before you got here, my only customer was me. Not *me* me but people that looked like me.

> **REESE**
> I know, that's what I'm here for—

> **OWNER**
> No no no. Listen. I used to think I was crazy. I'd look around, and there I'd be. By the cookbooks, the mysteries, the children's section. Little baby me's running all over the place. And my parents looked the same way. They looked like each other and the babies. They'd chase me through the store like they couldn't catch someone with six-inch legs. Reese, I couldn't catch a baby. But then you showed up.

> **REESE**
> I mean, I didn't just "show up."

You contacted me—

OWNER

And now look. We've got Blacks and
Spaniards. Chinese people. Islanders.

REESE

I get it—

OWNER

Muslims. Male, female. Homosexuals.
Transexuals.

REESE

I really think I should—

OWNER

Asexuals. Pansexuals. Native Ameri-
cans. Native American dwarfs.

REESE

Okay. See ya' next week!

Reese turns out of the alley, short of breath. They grab
a copy of the *Chicago Tribune* from a newspaper box,
then head into a nearby cafe.

INT. CAFE - CONTINUOUS

Reese nods to the cashier, then sits at a small table
beside a window. They cross their legs, unfold the
newspaper, and begin reading. After a moment, Reese
scans the room.

VAL, 50, clay head in the shape of a square, is sitting on the other side of the cafe, laughing. Val has wrinkles, but hides them with makeup. They are dressed in a nice silk shirt and slacks. They are wearing nail polish. Val has a feminine frame, but the voice of a man.

Reese squints and leans to get a better look. Across from Val is MATEUSZ, 40, a white male with a thick mustache, dressed in a dirty neon green T-shirt and paint-splattered cargo pants.

REESE

[Silently] What the fuck?

FADE OUT.

END OF ACT ONE

ACT TWO

FADE IN:

INT. SIMPLE CORP. - DAY

Bailey walks out of a cubicle, smelling their fingers. Behind them, an old Hispanic woman pulls her pants back up.

Bailey heads over to the *Ass Kisser* nameplate and stares out the window. They take a deep breath and rub their forehead.

Beside them, **BUTTON PUSHER #1**, 30s, a white male, and **BUTTON PUSHER #2**, 30s, an Asian female, are standing in front of the water fountain.

> **BUTTON PUSHER #1**
> It seems like that ass kisser's just back there licking me. My boxers are fuckin' drenched.

> **BUTTON PUSHER #2**
> That's better than no tongue! I feel like I have rug burn. Dry ass lips.

Bailey looks at them, they look at Bailey. Bailey goes back to looking out of the window.

> **INTERCOM**
> Ass Kisser to the boss's office. I repeat,
> Ass Kisser to the boss's office.

Bailey walks down an aisle to the boss's office. They peek inside cubicles filled with bored employees tapping big red buttons on their computer screens.

INT. BOSS'S OFFICE - CONTINUOUS

When Bailey opens the glass door, **THE BOSS**, late 20s, a white male with a man-bun, dressed in a suit, is sitting behind his massive desk. He double-clicks a button on his mouse and chillwave starts playing.

The office is full of ugly abstract art. There's a Newton's cradle with wrinkly balls pinging on his desk.

> **THE BOSS**
> Asslick! Come on in! Take a seat, take
> a seat.

Bailey sits.

> **THE BOSS**
> So, how's it goin' bud?

> **BAILEY**
> Not too bad. How about yourself?

THE BOSS
Not too bad indeed. How's the painting comin' along?

BAILEY
Um... I actually haven't gotten too much done lately. Work and all.

THE BOSS
Yeah... that'll happen. Only gets worse.

Prolonged eye contact and nodding. Bailey tries to help by laughing a little.

THE BOSS (CONT'D)
God. Could you imagine if you had to *pay* for that degree?

BAILEY
Yeah. I could imagine that.

THE BOSS
You would be hundreds of thousands of dollars in the hole. Not that you aren't already, eh?

Silence.

THE BOSS (CONT'D)
You smell like shit, but that's not why I called you into my office. You're here because... Well... I don't know how to put this, but uh... You're fired.

BAILEY
[Gulp] What?

THE BOSS
Too many demerits. The button-pushers just wish you were a little more enthusiastic, you know? Plus, you never comment on my music. I made this one.

The two of them listen to the shitty electronic muzak.

BAILEY
Okay.

Bailey starts to leave.

THE BOSS
Ha! I'm kidding! You should have seen your face!

Bailey blinks a couple of times. The Newton's cradle stops pinging.

THE BOSS (CONT'D)
Seriously, the real reason I called you in today is 'cause you're not wearing a name tag. You know the rules. Every button-pusher's gotta have one on.

The boss slides open a small drawer and pulls out a sparkly white name tag.

THE BOSS (CONT'D)
Wear it with pride, my friend. Sorry your name's not on it. Label maker's out of tape.

BAILEY
I... I don't know what to say. Thank you so much!

THE BOSS
You deserve it! Now go check out your new digs. You'll find that there's been some redecorating.

They shake hands and Bailey heads for the door.

THE BOSS
About the music... You could at least act interested. I work really hard on it.

INT. SIMPLE CORP. - CONTINUOUS

When Bailey leaves the boss's office, they jump in the air. *Hooray!* They pin the blank name tag over the coffee stain on their shirt and walk down the aisle, grinning. Bailey nods to the other button-pushers. Finger-guns. Gradually, they realize that none of the employees seem excited, but rather sad.

BUTTON PUSHER #3
Not you too.

There's a cubicle where the hook used to be. It's still weirdly isolated, and completely blocks the window. The nameplate on it reads: *B. Every*.

Bailey fondles the nameplate, smiles, then steps inside.

INT. GYMNASIUM - DAY

Blackness. Strobe lights pulse on Nicky, who has their head down.

Slowly, they start to move their shoulders as the music becomes more intense.

Red and blue lasers shoot through the gymnasium.

Nicky throws an arm in the air and shakes their hips. More lights hit them. With each shake, they inch closer to the floor. Soon, Nicky is on the floor, rolling around. They do the worm. Hump. Breakdance, though not very well.

They pop up and grab a basketball from the rack placed at half-court. The crowd goes wild.

Nicky runs toward a hoop, jumps on a spring, and gets rejected by the rim, falling onto their back with a thud. The crowd goes silent.

After a pause, Nicky is lifted up like an angel by an invisible harness. They start humping again.

They're swung all throughout the gym. When they get close enough to the bleachers, fans reach for them to no avail.

Nicky's brought back down to half-court. The music shifts to rap with a lot of bass. They go through every viral dance move.

The performance ends with Nicky outstretched over a chair, yanking a string which causes water to dump all over them.

The lights turn on. Nicky stands, bows. They look around and see everyone in the bleachers cheering. The closer they look, the more apparent it becomes that most people are just laughing.

Nicky heads to the sideline. The scoreboard reads: *Home: 12 Away: 86.*

Nicky stands beside Coach Nasso.

NICKY

How'd I do?

COACH NASSO

Are you kidding? Look around. Everyone loves you!

NICKY

[Beat] Coach?

COACH NASSO
What's up?

NICKY
I don't think I wanna—

COACH NASSO
Oh, hold that thought. Mr. Dumont! Mr.
Dumont! Wait! I thought we were gonna
grade papers together!

Coach Nasso runs after Mr. Dumont, who is leaving
with a female student.

Nicky scans the bleachers again. Most people are
leaving. Some are standing, waving. Nicky puts on a
smile and waves back.

INT. CAFE - DAY

Val smiles at Mateusz, who stares at his phone.
Mateusz has a heavy Eastern European accent.

MATEUSZ
Give one minute to me. Business of
work.

VAL
Remind me what you do again?

MATEUSZ
Construction. I drill. Hammer. Jack-
hammer. But before I am doing inter-
national spy.

VAL
Wow! That must've been hard.

MATEUSZ
You have no idea. Ha.

VAL
HA HA HA HA! How hard was it?

Mateusz looks up from his phone.

MATEUSZ
A lot.

Just then, Reese approaches.

REESE
Are you serious right now?

VAL
Reese! What are you doing here?

REESE
Working. What are you doing here?

VAL
Well... Mateusz and I are on a date.

REESE
Mateusz?

VAL
Yes, Mateusz. Mateusz, Reese. Reese,
Mateusz.

Mateusz sticks his left hand out. Reese looks at the hand, ignores it.

REESE
Val, we got divorced *last week.*

VAL
Yeah, I know. I was there.

REESE
So what are you thinking?

MATEUSZ
I am think of sex with this one.

Val blushes. Mateusz stands, and whispers in Reese's ear:

MATEUSZ
I no kid. Do I stick in or get stuck in? If stuck in is no problem, but I must have know before.

REESE
If you don't get the fuck out of my face, I'm gonna rip that mustache off.

MATEUSZ
[To Val] I go to washroom.

Mateusz leaves. Reese makes a gesture that says: *What the hell?* Val makes one that says: *So what?*

REESE

You knew I was gonna be here.

VAL

No I didn't.

REESE

Val.

VAL

What?

REESE

Come on.

VAL

Come on *what?* I'm not doing this here, Reese.

REESE

No one's doing anything. Just admit this whole thing is ridiculous.

VAL

I'm not sure what "thing" you're referring to. But if you're talking about Mateusz, he's actually a really nice—

REESE

I'm not talking about fuckin' Mateusz! I'm talking about *us*. This divorce. Val, I live at the Y.

VAL

You should have thought about that before you fucked my cousin!

REESE

Would you quiet down? I didn't fuck your cousin.

VAL

I know. [Beat] Look, are you coming over for dinner tonight? I'm making ground beef tacos.

FADE OUT.

<u>END OF ACT TWO</u>

<u>ACT THREE</u>

FADE IN:

INT. BAILEY'S CUBICLE - DAY

The cubicle has a desk, a desktop computer, and a rolling swivel chair.

Bailey is tilting back and forth in the chair, aggressively. They stop, then begin spinning around, their knees knocking against the desk with every revolution.

BAILEY

So much space! Goodness gracious. I could put a photo here. Hang a dreamcatcher there. [Beat] Oh shit. An easel! That is the perfect corner for an easel. A small one, but it'll grow. Mhm.

Bailey knocks on their desk. Once, twice, three times.

BAILEY

Hey, come on in! You're the new hire, huh? I'll tell you what, let's skip the whole "ass-kissing" thing. You don't have to worry about that in this cubicle. What's your name, kid?

They slouch and deepen their voice.

> **BAILEY**
> I think I'll uh... I think I'll switch it up today. Let's go *right* cheek. Feelin' spontaneous.

They man-spread and add a squeakiness to their voice.

> **BAILEY**
> I'm telling you right now, Ass Fuck, better not take another step if you forgot the goddamn feather again! I am not in the mood!

Bailey bursts into laughter.

> **BAILEY**
> This is crazy! Phew. Okay. Time to get serious.

They turn the hard drive on. A sharp white light and the sound of a gong emit from the monitor, startling Bailey. A large red button that says *PUSH* appears in the middle of the screen.

> **BAILEY**
> There it is. So many days, weeks, my whole life leading up to this one thing. It isn't even a thing. Things don't have names. But this, this has one. It's a button. If anything's a thing, it's me. [Beat] But that all ends here.

Bailey lifts their pointer finger, lets it hover in front of the button. Retracts it. Does this again, then pushes the button.

BAILEY
Oh!

They push the button again, then think about it for a moment. They push it again and again, picking up speed. With each push, Bailey becomes more aroused. Finally, Bailey climaxes.

BAILEY
I need to do that again.

Bailey pushes the button and a look of concern washes over them. They push some more.

BAILEY
[Continuously pushing] Hey, uh, Philip?
I think something's wrong with my computer. It doesn't feel... I don't know.
It kinda just feels like I'm poking glass.

No response.

BAILEY (CONT'D)
Glass. Ass. Asslick. Fuckin' stupid job.
What's this button even for?

The pushes become more forceful.

BAILEY (CONT'D)

Am I just pushing it to push it? Like, to occupy time? Is that what time's for? To occupy? Is this button keeping the lights on, the water running? Probably not. Kids aren't still starving, are they?

Pushes turn into punches.

BAILEY (CONT'D)

Kids. Piles of 'em. They're all dead. [Beat] What the fuck is this button for? Is it some World War Three shit? Am I killing people right now? Philip? Am I killing people? I hope so! I'd rather kill somebody than keep pushing some dumb broken button!

Bailey has completely destroyed the computer. Their hands are full of glass. They resort to stomping on it. They're flailing so much that the walls of the cubicle begin to crack and fall.

BAILEY

Just shut the fuck up! This is the best thing that's ever happened to you and you're ruining it! You always ruin things! Just shut up, *shut up!*

Bailey lifts what's left of the computer and hurls it at the window. Nothing. They try again and this time the window shatters. The computer falls, ending in a crash.

Heavy panting. After a pause, they turn around. All of their coworkers have gathered, staring.

BAILEY
I'll see myself out.

While grabbing their jacket, they can't help but overhear Button Pusher #1 and Button Pusher #2 by the water fountain:

BUTTON PUSHER #1
Can you believe that? What a fuckin' psycho.

BUTTON PUSHER #2
I know, right! It's probably because they're [whispers into #1's ear].

Button Pusher #1 laughs.

Bailey heads for the elevator. They press the button and wait. Just then, the boss approaches.

THE BOSS
Hey, uh... I just wanted to say, very punk rock. If it were up to me, you'd still have your job. Hell, if it were up to me, you'd have my job. Ha ha. But it's not. I'm just the boss, so...

Bailey steps into the elevator.

THE BOSS (CONT'D)
We should hang out sometime! You ever play Bo-taoshi? It's like capture the flag but super dope—

Bailey pushes the *door close* button a bunch of times. It doesn't work.

THE BOSS (CONT'D)
I get it. "The annoying boss." [Beat] Before you go, let me at least help you out real quick.

The boss hurries into the elevator before it closes. He approaches Bailey, who flinches. The boss pulls a marker out of his pocket.

When the elevator gets to the ground floor, the boss stays inside.

THE BOSS
I'll catch you Saturday, friend. *Bo-taoshi!*

Bailey ignores this. They walk past the man at the front desk, who waves. Bailey does not wave back.

When Bailey exits the building, they see the computer smashed on top of a car. They walk in the opposite direction.

INT. LOCKER ROOM - DAY

The basketball team is huddled together, defeated. Coach Nasso stands before them, drunk. Nicky lingers behind the players.

COACH NASSO

What'd ya' expect, ya' know? We were never that good to begin with. It's like—[Burp] Excuse me. It's like, so what if the other team's younger and prettier? Right? What about this team? We need to win sometimes too!

The players squint, scratch their heads.

COACH NASSO (CONT'D)

The other team's probably never even had a Pap smear. Like, go to the doctor.

PLAYER #1, mid teens, a boy in the front row, nudges his female teammate.

PLAYER #1

[Silently] The fuck is a Pap smear?

The teammate shrugs.

COACH NASSO (CONT'D)

But I do have some good news! Principal Bacarrezza has decided to give us some more money. I'm talkin' new uniforms. A tour bus. A little champagne during practice? All this thanks to our star mascot, Nicky!

Most of the players turn around and look at Nicky. A couple of them clap.

>COACH NASSO (CONT'D)
>Get ready to have that face of yours all over America!

Nicky smiles uncomfortably.

>COACH NASSO (CONT'D)
>Alright, everyone. Go home. Get some rest, because tomorrow this team is gonna make all these other teams look ugly as fuck.

The players start packing up.

>COACH NASSO (CONT'D)
>Nicky? Can I talk to you for a second?

Coach Nasso and Nicky find a private area of the locker room. Nicky starts to say something, but Coach Nasso cuts them off.

>COACH NASSO
>Before you say anything, I just wanted to thank you for doin' what you're doin'. I know sometimes you probably feel a little out of place and I can't even imagine the pressure, but you're doing a really great thing for your school, and I just wanted to let you know that I'm

here for you. So... What'd you wanna tell me?

                              NICKY
[Beat] I've never had champagne be-fore.

                         COACH NASSO
Ugh. You're gonna love it.

EXT. THE EVERY HOUSE - NIGHT

A bus stops, Nicky gets off. They run across the street, book bag swinging behind them. Nicky walks up the front steps of an old bungalow. They unlock the door and go inside.

INT. LIVING ROOM - CONTINUOUS

The living room is small, but nicely decorated. A lot of red and tan. There are dreamcatchers and leather couches. Two table lamps light the room. There's a cabinet full of knick-knacks, and a large TV. It's turned off.

There are voices coming from the kitchen, but Nicky ignores them. They put their book bag down and grab a teen magazine off of the front room table. Underneath it, there's a past due bill for three hundred dollars.

Nicky walks upstairs, skimming the magazine. They go into their room, flip the light on. It's extremely messy.

52

The walls are filled with posters ranging from Chief Keef to Ariana Grande, Dali paintings to Rupi Kaur poems.

They plop down on their bed, tossing the magazine on the floor. [Beat] They stand, then approach a full-length mirror.

Nicky pulls up their sleeves, examines their arms. Touches their neck. Tugs at their face a bit.

The tugs become more violent. Soon, Nicky is scratching their face. Slivers of clay get stuck in their nails. One thin stream of blood trickles down their cheek.

When Nicky realizes that their face isn't coming off:

> **NICKY**
> Fuck!

They sink to the floor and begin to cry.

INT. KITCHEN - NIGHT

Bailey, Nicky, Reese, and Val are sitting at the kitchen table. In front of them, a platter of ground beef tacos.

> **VAL**
> So... How was everyone's day?

Bailey is expressionless. They're still wearing the name tag, which reads: *Bailey*, written in marker.

Nicky is defeated. One side of their face is completely torn.

Reese is stuffing food in their mouth.

> **VAL (CONT'D)**
> Okay. Since no one wants to answer, I have big news! Remember how I signed up for Ancestry.com? Well, I got the results!

> **BAILEY**
> And?

> **VAL**
> I haven't looked yet. I'm too nervous.

> **BAILEY**
> How much did you pay for that thing?

> **VAL**
> A hundred bucks.

> **BAILEY**
> You do realize that it's a scam, right?

> **VAL**
> How?

> **BAILEY**
> Everyone's from Africa.

> **VAL**
> Where in Africa?

> **BAILEY**
> Ethiopia, I think.

> **VAL**
> Do I *look* Ethiopian to you?

> **BAILEY**
> You look... Cuban.

The kids laugh, then Val joins in.

> **VAL**
> This is serious stuff!

> **REESE**
> Can I just say something? [To Bailey and Nicky] Watchin' you two right now... Words can't even begin to describe how proud I am. [To Val] We raised 'em well. And I know we haven't seen eye-to-eye lately, but you all are my family and no matter what happens, I just want you to know—

Just then, Mateusz comes out of the bedroom wearing nothing but underwear. He grabs a handful of ground beef and scarfs it down. He kisses Val on top of the head, then retreats back into the room, shutting the door behind him.

Val cracks a smile that soon fades.

The family eats in silence.

FADE OUT.

<u>THE END</u>

Acknowledgements

First and foremost, thank you Mom and Dad for all your support, and the sacrifices you made that allowed me to even think of writing this book. A big thanks to Clare Boland and Audie Shushan for the invaluable feedback. Thank you Jenny Boully and José Olivarez for your kind words! Many thanks to Joshua Bohnsack and Joseph Demes for believing in this script. And all the thanks in the world to my wife, Abbey, for the help, help, *help*.

A Note on the Text

The body of this text was set in Arial designed by Robin Nicholas and Patricia Saunders in 1982. The ornamental text was set in Karrik, created by Jean-Baptiste Morizot and Lucas Le Bihan in 2020.

Long Day Press

New & Forthcoming Titles

Whimsy
Shannon McLeod
Novella
ISBN: 9781950987108 • $14

Love Stories & Other Love Stories
Justin Brouckaert
Stories
ISBN: 9781950987115 • $14

Rain Revolutions
Bessie Flores Zaldívar
Stories
ISBN: 9781950987177 • $14

What's On the Menu?
Chase Griffin
Novella
ISBN: 9781950987016 • $14

LongDayPress.com **@LongDayPress**